AF228582

PROFESSIONAL SPORTS LEAGUES

NBA

BY WILL GRAVES

CONTENT CONSULTANT
Stew Thornley
Sports Historian
Author of *Minnesota Hoops: Basketball in the North Star State*

Essential Library
An Imprint of Abdo Publishing | abdobooks.com

ABDOBOOKS.COM

Published by Abdo Publishing, a division of ABDO, PO Box 398166, Minneapolis, Minnesota 55439. Copyright © 2021 by Abdo Consulting Group, Inc. International copyrights reserved in all countries. No part of this book may be reproduced in any form without written permission from the publisher. Essential Library™ is a trademark and logo of Abdo Publishing.

Printed in the United States of America, North Mankato, Minnesota.
042020
092020

Cover Photos: Rick Bowmer/AP Images, foreground; Tony Avelar/AP Images, background
Interior Photos: Stephen Lew/Icon Sportswire/AP Images, 4 , 13 (background), 14–15 (background), 18 (background), 26–27 (background), 32 (background), 36–37 (background), 43 (background), 46, 54 (background), 60–61 (background), 70, 82–83 (background), 90–91 (background), 95 (background); Eric Risberg/AP Images, 5, 10, 53; Red Line Editorial, 13 (chart), 43 (chart), 95 (chart); Bettmann/Getty Images, 15, 94; Chiang Ying-ying/AP Images, 18 (foreground); Charles Knoblock/AP Images, 21; Brian Rothmuller/Icon Sportswire/AP Images, 24; AP Images, 26–27 (foreground), 32, 35, 39, 71, 74; Sam Myers/AP Images, 30; Richard Mackson/Sports Illustrated/Set Number: X29664 TK1 R13/Getty Images, 36–37 (foreground); John Swart/AP Images, 47; Charlie Knoblock/AP Images, 49; Susan Ragan/AP Images, 54 (foreground); Mark J. Terrill/AP Images, 58; Mark Duncan/AP Images, 60–61 (foreground); Ann Heisenfelt/AP Images, 66; Marcio Jose Sanchez/AP Images, 68; Paul Connors/AP Images, 79; Dave Pickoff/AP Images, 82–83; Ron Frehm/AP Images, 87, 88; Paul Vathis/AP Images, 90–91 (foreground); John W. McDonough/Sports Illustrated/Set Number: X162610 TK1/Getty Images, 99

Editor: Arnold Ringstad
Series Designer: Dan Peluso

LIBRARY OF CONGRESS CONTROL NUMBER: 2019954200
PUBLISHER'S CATALOGING-IN-PUBLICATION DATA
Names: Graves, Will, author.
Title: NBA / by Will Graves
Description: Minneapolis, Minnesota : Abdo Publishing, 2021 | Series: Professional sports leagues | Includes online resources and index.
Identifiers: ISBN 9781532192081 (lib. bdg.) | ISBN 9781532179983 (ebook)
Subjects: LCSH: National Basketball Association--Juvenile literature. | Basketball--Juvenile literature. | Professional sports franchises--Juvenile literature. | Sports--United States--History--Juvenile literature.
Classification: DDC 796.32364--dc23

CONTENTS

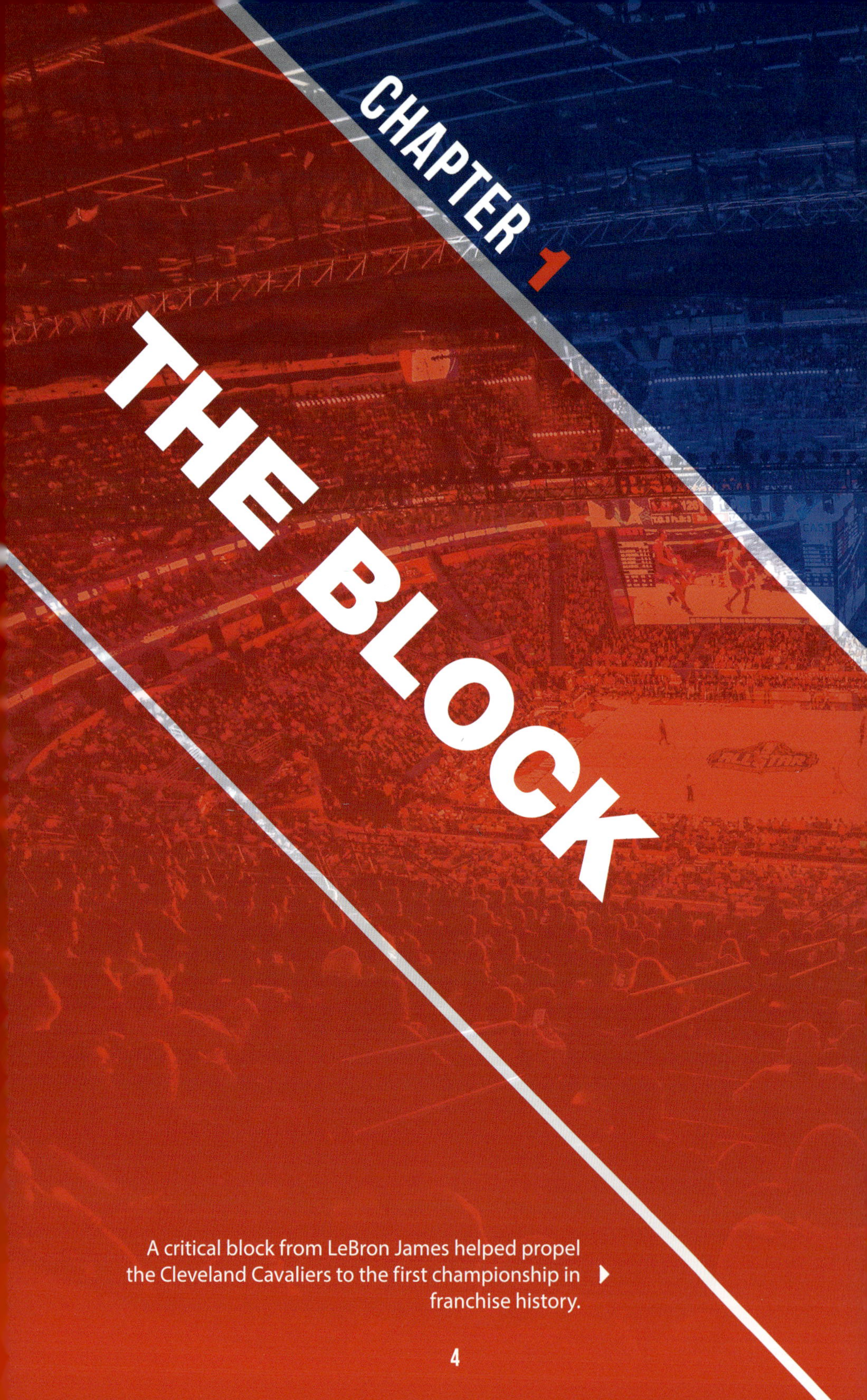

A critical block from LeBron James helped propel the Cleveland Cavaliers to the first championship in franchise history. ▶

SPALDING
JAMES
23
IGUODALA
9

ndre Iguodala had the ball in his hands and a second
straight NBA title for his Golden State Warriors in his
sights. The one thing the veteran forward didn't see was
LeBron James of the Cleveland Cavaliers. There were two
minutes left in the fourth quarter of Game 7 of the 2016 NBA
Finals. The championship series seemed destined to end
with the Warriors taking the lead and the championship,
and James was nowhere to be found.

In fact, the Cavaliers star had been three or four steps
behind Iguodala when the veteran Golden State forward
grabbed the rebound. With the score tied, Iguodala spotted
teammate Steph Curry racing up the court. Iguodala flipped
a pass to Curry. While Curry dribbled down the court,
Iguodala raced to the Golden State hoop.

When Iguodala reached the lane, Curry found him with
a perfect bounce pass. The only thing between Iguodala
and the go-ahead bucket was Cleveland Cavaliers guard
J. R. Smith. Iguodala took two steps to get around Smith
and leaped for a layup. Then what will forever be known as
"The Block" happened. As Iguodala flipped the ball toward
the hoop, James appeared out of nowhere. He extended
his arms to smack the ball off the backboard and away from
the hoop. The incredible play helped James deliver on his
promise to bring Cleveland a championship at last.

A GOLDEN OPPORTUNITY MISSED

In a flash, Golden State's dream of finishing off the most incredible season in NBA history was in serious danger of disappearing. The Warriors entered the 2016 Finals with a chance to stake a claim as the best basketball team ever. Golden State had won the 2015 Finals with a relatively easy victory over James and the Cavaliers. The Warriors were even better in 2016. They set a league record with 73 wins during the regular season behind stars Curry and Klay Thompson. The duo was known as "The Splash Brothers" for their ability to knock down three-point shots.

Golden State faced a challenge in the Western Conference finals, trailing Kevin Durant and the Oklahoma City Thunder three games to one in the best-of-seven series. The Warriors surged back to capture the series in seven games and then raced to a three-games-to-one lead against Cleveland in the finals.

But Warriors center Draymond Green ran into trouble near the end of Game 4 when he punched James after the two players got tangled up on the court. The officials called Green for a flagrant foul. As part of his punishment, Green was suspended for Game 5.

With the Warriors missing one of the best defensive players in the NBA, Cleveland pounced. The Cavaliers cruised to a 15-point win in Game 5. Then the teams went to Cleveland for Game 6. The rowdy home fans at Quicken Loans Arena helped push the Cavaliers to a quick 22-point lead. Golden State never recovered, and Cleveland's 115–101 victory set up a winner-take-all Game 7.

WINNER TAKE ALL

Game 7 was tightly contested, but when Iguodala broke into the open with the score knotted at 89, the Warriors appeared ready to celebrate in front of a raucous home crowd at Oracle Arena in Oakland, California. The Block changed all that. It was a play that left Iguodala shaking his head. Iguodala knew he had done everything right. But so had James. "I mean, I wouldn't have changed anything about it," Iguodala said. "If somebody just makes a great play, you just give them respect for making a great play."[2]

It wasn't the last one for the Cavaliers. Point guard Kyrie Irving gave Cleveland the lead for good with a tough three-pointer with 53 seconds to go. With Curry guarding him, Irving dribbled the ball between his own legs just outside the three-point line. Curry lunged at the ball as Irving pulled up for a jump shot. Curry missed. Irving did not. The ball swished through the net to give the Cavaliers a 92–89 lead.

The Warriors never scored again. Golden State missed their final nine shots of the game, including a three-point attempt by Curry with 31 seconds left that would have tied the game. James made a free throw to push Cleveland's advantage to 93–89 with 11 seconds left. Two more desperate three-point heaves by Golden State clanked off the rim. When the final buzzer sounded, the Cavaliers poured onto the floor in celebration after becoming the first

James held both the championship trophy and his most valuable player trophy during the team's emotional celebration.

team ever to rally from a 3–1 deficit to win the Finals and just the fourth team to ever win a Game 7 on the road.

James was in the middle of it all. The player known as King James finished Game 7 with 27 points, 11 rebounds, 11 assists, and three blocks. No block was bigger than the one that denied Iguodala and set the stage for Cleveland's first pro sports championship since 1964. The victory fulfilled James's longtime promise to the Cavaliers. James said he'd one day bring Cleveland a title. After his four-year stint with the Miami Heat in the early 2010s, he returned to Cleveland in 2014. "I came back for a reason," James said. "I came back to bring a championship to our city. I knew what I was capable of doing."[3]

A LASTING MEMORY

Cleveland's losses to the Warriors were tough. They would go on to lose the 2017 and 2018 Finals to the Warriors. Still, they'll always have the 2016 Finals, when the game's greatest player delivered in the biggest moment of his career. It was a moment shared by fans across the United States. More than 44 million people watched the last seconds tick off the clock, a sign of just how popular the NBA had become.[4]

A league that spent its early days in the 1940s playing in a handful of American cities has grown into one of the most popular and widespread sports leagues in the world. Today's NBA features 30 teams, including one in Toronto, Canada. The league's top stars come from all over the planet, whether it's Akron, Ohio, like

James or Athens, Greece, like 2019 NBA most valuable player (MVP) Giannis Antetokounmpo. And every winter and spring, NBA arenas are jam-packed with fans who roar at every high-arcing three-pointer and rim-shaking dunk.

There's still room in the NBA, though, for a little defense—look no further than "The Block" for proof. The biggest play of James's career happened thanks to a mix of hustle and talent. With one swing of his arms, James changed the course of basketball history and provided a play that will live in NBA lore forever. "I don't know how I got there," James said. "But I'm grateful that I did."[5]

THE NBA'S STRUCTURE

WESTERN CONFERENCE

NORTHWEST DIVISION

Denver Nuggets
Minnesota Timberwolves
Oklahoma City Thunder
Portland Trail Blazers
Utah Jazz

PACIFIC DIVISION

Golden State Warriors
Los Angeles Clippers
Los Angeles Lakers
Phoenix Suns
Sacramento Kings

SOUTHWEST DIVISION

Dallas Mavericks
Houston Rockets
Memphis Grizzlies
New Orleans Pelicans
San Antonio Spurs

EASTERN CONFERENCE

ATLANTIC DIVISION

Boston Celtics
Brooklyn Nets
New York Knicks
Philadelphia 76ers
Toronto Raptors

CENTRAL DIVISION

Chicago Bulls
Cleveland Cavaliers
Detroit Pistons
Indiana Pacers
Milwaukee Bucks

SOUTHEAST DIVISION

Atlanta Hawks
Charlotte Hornets
Miami Heat
Orlando Magic
Washington Wizards

CHAPTER 2

A MODEST BEGINNING

After inventing the sport, James Naismith was the head coach of the University of Kansas's first basketball team. ▶ He died in 1939, too early to see the founding of the NBA.

Professional basketball is a global game these days. The United States, China, Italy, Australia, and Brazil are among the countries with professional leagues. It's a far cry from the game's humble roots, when a gym teacher at Springfield College in Springfield, Massachusetts, named James Naismith was asked to come up with an activity to keep his students busy during the cold New England winters.

In 1891, Naismith created a game that borrowed a little bit from football and a little bit from soccer, adding a dash of other sports, such as field hockey. He placed a peach basket ten feet (3 m) off the ground and required players to work together to shoot a ball into it. Naismith used two words to describe his new game: "basket ball."[1] He came up with 13 rules for his new game.[2] Some are still in place today. Players still have only five seconds to throw the ball in after it goes out of bounds.

Basketball grew quickly as Naismith's students spread the word about the exciting new game. The first professional league, the National Basketball League (NBL), formed in 1898 but folded within a few years. Interest in professional basketball lagged behind interest in games at the high school or college level. There were, however, exceptions. A team called the Original Celtics was formed in 1914 in New York City. Over the next decade they were nearly unbeatable. Led by stars Nat Holman and Joe

Lapchick, the Celtics were professional basketball's first
dominant team. During one national tour, they posted
a record of 193–11–1. The Celtics joined the American
Basketball League (ABL) in the 1920s. But they were too
good. The ABL kicked them out after the Celtics won the
title in 1926 and 1927. Professional basketball continued to
increase in popularity.

The ABL went out of business in 1930. The National Basketball League (NBL), unrelated to the earlier league of the same name, arrived in 1937 to take its place. The NBL began with 13 teams, most of them located in the Midwest. Some cities struggled to keep teams. The Buffalo Bisons lasted just one season. More than 35 different teams played at least one season in the NBL during its 12-year run, proof that the league had trouble finding sustained fan support.[3]

Up in Boston, Massachusetts, Walter Brown couldn't help but notice fans' appetite for pro basketball. Brown owned

HARLEM
GLOBETROTTERS

One of the most important people in the early days of professional basketball never played an actual game. Abe Saperstein was a 24-year-old businessman who started promoting a team of players he called the Savoy Big Five in 1926. The team got its name from the Savoy Ballroom, a music and sports venue in Chicago. Saperstein kept changing the name of his team in the early days, eventually settling on the Harlem Globetrotters.

The Globetrotters really did trot all over the globe, winning wherever they went. Sometimes the Globetrotters would be winning by so much, they'd start goofing off late in games. The crowd ate it up, and soon their on-court antics became a regular part of each contest. The Globetrotters became ambassadors for the game all over the world, a tradition that continues to this day. The Globetrotters have played in more than 120 countries and territories all over the world, spreading basketball and laughter wherever they go.[4]

The Globetrotters entertain audiences with a mix of physical comedy and basketball skill.

Boston Garden, a famous arena in the city's downtown area. He saw how the NBL had found a way to stay in business and thought it was time to bring pro hoops to bigger cities.

Brown gathered together businessmen from places such as New York City; Washington, DC; Philadelphia, Pennsylvania; Chicago, Illinois; and Cleveland, Ohio, to establish the Basketball Association of America (BAA). The BAA debuted with 11 clubs in 1946. The teams played in modern arenas like the Garden in Boston and Madison Square Garden in New York. Just like the NBL, though, the BAA had trouble finding support. Only eight teams suited up for the league's second season. Maurice Podoloff, chosen by the league owners to be the BAA's first commissioner,

THE NEW YORK RENS BREAK BARRIERS

Professional basketball's first real rivalry might have been between the Original Celtics and the New York Renaissance, also known as the Rens. The Rens were the first all-black professional team. Founded in the Harlem neighborhood of New York City in the 1920s, the Rens played a fast-paced style that dared their opponents to keep up. Most of them couldn't. The Rens were one of basketball's first super teams. They won 88 straight games in the span of 86 days in 1932–33 and in 1939 captured the first World Professional Tournament Championship.[5] The Rens wanted to play in a professional league, but none of the leagues at the time allowed black players. So the Rens were forced to barnstorm instead, going on exhibition tours from city to city to take on local teams. They helped prove basketball players could be great regardless of skin color. The Rens won more than 2,000 games before disbanding in 1949.[6]

soon realized the BAA's biggest problem. The BAA lacked the one thing it needed the most: basketball's best player.

GEORGE MIKAN AND THE BIRTH OF THE NBA

George Mikan was basketball's first true superstar. The six-foot-ten center towered over opponents while playing at DePaul University in Chicago. Wearing his famous No. 99 jersey and sporting glasses that made him look more like a teacher than one of the world's top athletes, Mikan was nearly unstoppable. Fans flocked to watch him block shots at one end of the court and drop in basket after basket at the other with his famous hook shot. After graduating from DePaul, Mikan decided to stay in Chicago and play for the NBL's Chicago American Gears. He averaged 16.5 points per game as a rookie in 1946–47 while helping the Gears to the NBL title. Mikan moved on to the Minneapolis Lakers the following season and was even better, leading the league with 21.3 points per game and guiding the Lakers to the championship.

Podoloff understood that for the BAA to survive, it needed Mikan. So Podoloff approached the owners of four NBL teams in 1948 and talked them into joining the BAA. "What we had, he wanted—the superstars of that time," Rochester Royals owner Les Harrison said. "And what he

Mikan's height helped him dominate professional basketball in the late 1940s and early 1950s.

had we wanted—Madison Square Garden and the other big arenas."[7]

Mikan was an instant hit. During one game against the New York Knicks at Madison Square Garden, the sign out front read simply, "Geo. Mikan vs. Knicks." When Mikan walked into the locker room for the game, his teammates on the Lakers were dressed in regular clothes. They joked with their star, telling him, "They're advertising you're playing against the Knicks, so go play them. We'll wait here."[8]

With Mikan manning the middle, the Lakers steamrolled their way to the BAA title in their first season in the league in 1949. With Mikan now in the BAA, the NBL had trouble staying in business. Before the 1949–50 season, the remaining teams decided to join Mikan and the Lakers in the BAA. But the combined 17-team league needed a new name. On August 3, 1949, the National Basketball Association (NBA) was born.

THE FABULOUS FIFTIES

The NBA faced challenges in its early years. Thankfully, the league had Mikan to help lead the way. The Minneapolis Lakers were the NBA's first dynasty. With Mikan patrolling the lane, the Lakers won five NBA championships between 1949 and 1954. Mikan was so good, the new league was forced to change a rule to make it fair for other teams. The NBA widened the lane from six feet (1.8 m) to 12 feet (3.7 m) so Mikan couldn't just stand in the middle of the floor, block shots at one end, and make easy baskets at the other.

The league made other changes in this era, too. It adopted a 24-second shot clock so teams would be forced to shoot. Mikan had some influence on this change. During a game between the Lakers and the Fort Wayne Pistons in 1950, the Pistons decided the best way to beat Mikan and the Lakers was to keep the ball away from the star player. So the Pistons held on to the ball for long stretches, passing it from one side of the court to the other and refusing to put up a shot.

The fans had paid to watch Mikan and the Lakers play basketball, not just stand around, so they were not happy. Those who stuck around to the end at Minneapolis Auditorium booed. Even the referees encouraged the Pistons to shoot the ball to keep the game moving. Fort Wayne refused. The strategy worked. Fort Wayne won 19–18 in the lowest scoring game in NBA history.

Soon, other teams adopted Fort Wayne's strategy, usually at the end of a game or in overtime. A full-game stall didn't happen again, but the overall pace of play slowed. Instead of high-flying fast breaks, the conclusions of games turned into snooze-fests. Interest in the new league faded quickly. By 1954, the number of teams had dropped from 17 to nine. The NBA was in danger of going the way of the NBL and all the other pro basketball leagues that failed to stick.

In today's NBA, the shot clock is located directly above each basket, below the game clock.

A SHOT IN THE ARM

Something needed to be done. In August 1954, a group that included Boston Celtics coach Red Auerbach got together in Syracuse, New York, home of the Syracuse Nationals. They came up with an idea that changed not only the NBA but basketball all over the world. They called it the shot clock. The new rule required a team to put up a shot 24 seconds or less after getting the ball. There would be no more standing around, and no more putting the fans to sleep.

The shot clock was an instant hit. Scoring went up immediately. The game became more entertaining. Teams could no longer hog the ball to protect their leads. They had to keep playing until the final whistle, giving opponents a chance to come back. It's a lesson the Fort Wayne

Pistons painfully learned while facing Syracuse in the 1955
NBA Finals.

Early in the second quarter of Game 7, Fort Wayne was
up by 17 points. Under the old rules, the Pistons could have
done next to nothing and cruised to a championship. The
shot clock, however, required the Pistons to keep shooting.
They started missing, and Syracuse eventually caught up.
The Nationals rallied for a 92–91 victory to claim the title.

The shot clock gave the NBA an identity, something
that set it apart from the college game. Over the next few
years, word spread about the exciting brand of basketball in
the pro league. By 1958, teams were averaging 106 points
per game. And just as important, the stands were full.
Attendance rose by 40 percent between 1954 and 1958.[9]
Nearly 70 years after James Naismith introduced the game
in a Massachusetts gym, professional basketball was clearly
here to stay.

A STAR-STUDDED AFFAIR

The NBA added an All-Star Game during the 1950–51 season as a way
to showcase its best players. A crowd of more than 10,000 filled Boston
Garden to watch Ed Macauley of the hometown Boston Celtics capture
the game's most valuable player award after scoring 20 points to lead
the East to a 111–94 win over the West.[10] The All-Star Game has grown
to become All-Star Weekend, which features the Slam Dunk Contest,
a three-point shooting contest, and a skills contest the night before
the game.

THE BASKETBALL BOOM

Arnold "Red" Auerbach, *right*, coached many legendary stars in his career, including Bob Cousy.

The NBA needed a new face after Mikan stepped away for good in the mid-1950s at age 31. Thankfully for the league, it found one in Boston Celtics coach Arnold "Red" Auerbach. Auerbach grew up in New York City, played college ball at George Washington University in the early 1940s, and then started coaching at the end of World War II (1939–1945). He was out of work in the summer of 1950 when Celtics owner Walter Brown offered him a job leading the team. The decision changed the course of the NBA.

Auerbach had an eye for talent and wasn't afraid to make bold decisions. Shortly after taking over in Boston, he made Duquesne University guard Chuck Cooper the first African-American to be drafted into the NBA when the Celtics selected Cooper in the second round of the 1950 draft. The decision opened the NBA's doors to players of all races and sent the message that the league was open to the best players in the world, regardless of color.

Auerbach was just getting started. While the Celtics won plenty of games early in Auerbach's time on the bench, Boston usually fell short in the playoffs. The Celtics played a speedy style of basketball led by flashy point guard Bob Cousy. What Boston lacked was a big man in the middle to anchor the defense. Auerbach acted boldly. He sent forward Ed Macauley and the rights to small forward Cliff Hagan to the St. Louis Hawks in exchange for the second pick in the draft, giving him the chance to get Bill Russell.

The six-foot-ten Russell's arrival turned Boston into a powerhouse. It also provided the NBA with what it needed: a highly successful team in a major city. The Celtics didn't just win after Russell hopped on board. They dominated. Boston won the championship 11 times during a 13-year stretch from 1957 to 1969, including eight consecutive titles from 1959 through 1966. No franchise before or since has come close to challenging the Celtics' dynasty. Raising a championship banner to the rafters at Boston Garden became a ritual nearly every fall.

RUSSELL'S RISE

After leading Boston to an eighth straight title in 1966, Auerbach decided to step away from coaching to focus on his job as the team's general manager. Russell didn't want his coach to leave. He called Auerbach's wife and told her he didn't want to play for any coach other than Auerbach.

Bill Russell (6) went on to win 11 NBA championships in a 13-year career.

Auerbach wouldn't budge. So Russell came up with an idea. What if he took over for Auerbach and kept playing at the same time? It was an idea Auerbach couldn't resist. "I said to myself, 'Who could better motivate Bill Russell than Bill Russell?'" Auerbach recalled.[1]

Russell became the first African American coach in NBA history. But his first season in 1966–67 didn't turn out as planned. For the first time in nearly a decade, Boston didn't win the NBA title. The Celtics didn't even reach the Finals, losing to the Philadelphia 76ers in the Eastern Conference finals. Some thought Boston's time as the NBA's gold

standard was done. Philadelphia fans put together a sign
that read "Boston is Dead."[2] They were wrong.

Though the Celtics were getting older, Russell guided
them back to the top. Boston survived three hard-fought
playoff series to capture the championship in 1968. A
year later, the Celtics went 48–34 during the regular
season, their lowest win total since 1957, when the teams
played just 72 games in a season instead of 82. When the
postseason started, the Celtics found a second wind. Boston
reached the NBA Finals, where the star-laden Los Angeles
Lakers awaited.

The Lakers were led by guard Jerry West and center
Wilt Chamberlain. Boston trailed three games to two in the
best-of-seven series, but they pulled out a 99–90 victory
in Game 6 to force a Game 7. Knowing it would be his final

WILT
CHAMBERLAIN

Wilt Chamberlain could have been a star in many sports. Though he eventually grew to seven feet one, he was just as comfortable on a track as he was on the basketball court. He won a conference title in the high jump during his college days at the University of Kansas.

Basketball, however, is where Chamberlain truly dominated. The man known as the Big Dipper was unstoppable on the court. He averaged 30.1 points per game during his 14-year career. During the 1961–62 season, he poured in 50.4 points a game, the highest ever scoring average in a single season. By the time he retired in 1973, he had scored 31,419 points, the most ever by any player at the time. The only thing Chamberlain couldn't do with relative ease during his 14-year career was beat Russell. They squared off eight times in the playoffs, with Chamberlain's team winning just once.

Chamberlain broke the single-season scoring record in 1962, scoring 4,029 points. He celebrated with the ball used to break the record after the game.

time on the court as a player, the 34-year-old Russell was determined to leave the same way he came in: as a winner. Though he scored just six points, he grabbed 21 rebounds, and the Celtics held on for a 108–106 victory. Boston's win was a fitting tribute to Russell's legacy. He played ten winner-take-all Game 7s in his career, and he won all ten of them. "People say there were better teams than the Celtics," Russell said. "But we set the standard. A given team might come up for a year, but only we could sustain it."[3]

A NEW RIVAL

When Russell entered the NBA, there were just eight teams in the league. When he left, there were 14—the NBA had caught on across the country. Pro basketball became so popular that a new league popped up in 1967 to challenge the NBA.

The American Basketball Association (ABA) wanted to be different. It ditched a traditional orange basketball in favor of one that was red, white, and blue. The ABA adopted a three-point line long before it became a part of the NBA, and it held the first slam dunk contest. The league even hired George Mikan, the NBA's first star, to serve as its first commissioner.

The ABA paid big money to college stars. Some of the greatest players of all time began their careers there, while others left the NBA for the new league. Guard Rick Barry left the NBA's Warriors to join the ABA's Oakland Oaks. Artis Gilmore powered the Kentucky Colonels. No player in the upstart league soared higher than Julius Erving.

Nicknamed Dr. J, Erving was known for high-flying dunks for the Virginia Squires and the New York Nets. His stunning moves gave the basketball world a jolt. Before Erving came along, the dunk was just the easiest way to score two points. Erving turned dunking into an art form. In the first slam dunk contest, held before the 1976 ABA All-Star Game, Erving ran the length of the court, took off at the foul line 15 feet (4.6 m) from the basket, and appeared to fly toward the hoop before jamming the ball through the net. The crowd roared in approval.

Though the ABA merged with the NBA in 1976 when the Denver Nuggets, the Indiana Pacers, the San Antonio Spurs, and the Nets joined the league, the ABA's legacy lives on. Erving's arrival in 1976 put the NBA on track to reach the same heights of popularity as the National Football League

Erving's high-flying dunks wowed fans in the ABA before he joined the NBA for the last decade of his career.

and Major League Baseball. Thirty years after its creation, the NBA was almost ready to reach a new level. It just needed a touch of Magic.

BIRD AND MAGIC

Larry Bird, *left*, and Magic Johnson became the faces of the NBA in the 1980s.

CELTICS
33
LAKERS
32

Julius Erving could do a lot of things with a basketball. His hands were so large he could grab a ball and squeeze it like an orange. He could thunder down the lane for a dunk or swoop under the basket for a graceful layup. In many ways, he was the NBA's first made-for-TV superstar. He had the good looks, the smile, and most important, the skills to bring fans to the arena. He played first for the New York Nets and then for the Philadelphia 76ers, who brought Dr. J in before the 1976–77 season. The one thing Erving couldn't do was take the NBA to the next level by himself, no matter how great a player he was. He needed help. And in the winter of 1979, it arrived.

A TALE OF TWO STARS

A tall point guard from Michigan State University landed in Los Angeles at the same time a skinny small forward from Indiana arrived in Boston. On October 12, 1979, Earvin "Magic" Johnson took the court for the first time for the Lakers. That same night, on the other side of the country, Larry Bird suited up for the Celtics. And in an instant, the NBA changed forever.

On the surface, the two players most responsible for turning the NBA into a global game couldn't be more different. The six-foot-nine Johnson was unlike any player in league history. He saw the game differently than those who came before him. His court vision, the ability to see all the

Johnson amazed basketball fans in high school and college, and his excellence continued into the NBA.

players on the court and decide quickly where to go with the ball, was amazing.

A sportswriter gave him the nickname Magic when Johnson was still in high school, after watching him score 36 points while also getting 16 rebounds and 16 assists. There were great scorers before Johnson came along. There had been great rebounders and passers, too. But there wasn't anyone else who could do all of them at the same time and with the same flash that Johnson provided on a nightly basis.

Except, perhaps, for Larry Bird. Bird grew up a skinny teenager with a wispy mustache from tiny French Lick, Indiana. Like Johnson, Bird stood six feet nine and could rebound, pass, and shoot with ease. But unlike Johnson, Bird did not seem to welcome the spotlight. Where Johnson was loud, Bird was quiet. Where Johnson's electric smile seemed to only get brighter the more cameras captured his every move, Bird didn't particularly care either way.

The two players were already household names when they arrived in the NBA in the fall of 1979. They had become well-known as fans followed their college careers. Johnson and Bird met in the 1979 national championship game before turning pro. A record-sized television audience watched as Johnson and Michigan State held off Bird and Indiana State 75–64. There was something about the way Johnson and Bird played that drew fans in. "Bird and Magic brought passing back into the game," said former coach and TV commentator Al Maguire. "Back then, all the publicity went to the slam-dunkers and the gunners. But these two guys showed you could be unselfish and still be a star."[1]

A LUCKY FLIP

The NBA anxiously awaited the arrival of Bird and Johnson. Bird was already slated to join the Celtics, who selected him in the 1978 NBA Draft and were then forced to wait while he played one more year at Indiana State. Johnson was the clear top choice in the 1979 draft. The New Orleans Jazz had the first overall pick. Unfortunately for the Jazz, they owed their pick to the Lakers due to an earlier deal.

Los Angeles nabbed Johnson, and the two proved to be a perfect match. He created a brand of basketball that caught the imagination of fans across the world. The Lakers called it "Showtime."[2] The phrase didn't come from Johnson but from team owner Jerry Buss. Buss wanted his team to play a style that would make the movie stars in nearby Hollywood want to sit courtside while Johnson did his thing. People came to the Great Western Forum for Lakers home games not only to watch Johnson but also to catch a glimpse of the celebrities who were there to see the action. Johnson's electric presence made it hard to look away from the court. "Showtime" was no-look passes. It was frantic

MOVE OVER WILT

Kareem Abdul-Jabbar might be the most graceful big man in NBA history. The 7-foot-2 center didn't use brute force to overpower opponents. Instead, he used his knowledge of the game and an unstoppable sky hook to dominate. Abdul-Jabbar's signature shot was impossible to block. On April 5, 1984, he used it to break Wilt Chamberlain's all-time career scoring record. With his back to the basket, Abdul-Jabbar extended his right arm high over his head and released a skyhook over the outstretched arms of 7-foot-4 Utah center Mark Eaton. The ball swished through the net for his 31,420th career point, one more than Chamberlain. Abdul-Jabbar finished with 38,387 career points, a record that still stands.

fast breaks. It was Johnson running down the court with the ball in his hands and his imagination at work.

Johnson's impact on the Lakers was immediate. Los Angeles won the NBA title during Johnson's rookie season in 1979–80, beating Julius Erving and the Philadelphia 76ers in six games. In Game 6, Johnson put on a performance unlike any in NBA history. The Lakers were without center Kareem Abdul-Jabbar, who was forced to sit out with an ankle injury. So Johnson started at center in Abdul-Jabbar's place. The rookie finished with 42 points, 15 rebounds, and seven assists, making all 14 of his free throws along the way. He was named the most valuable player of the Finals.

A BOSTON REVIVAL

Like Johnson's in Los Angeles, Bird's arrival in Boston gave the Celtics an immediate boost. Boston finished 61–21 in Bird's rookie season in 1979–80, more than double the team's win total from the previous year. Bird beat out Johnson for the NBA's Rookie of the Year award, averaging 21.3 points, 10.4 rebounds, and 4.5 assists. It marked the

LARRY BIRD

"MAGIC" JOHNSON

LARRY BIRD		"MAGIC" JOHNSON
1979–1992	**SEASONS PLAYED**	1979–1991; 1995–1996
21,791	**TOTAL POINTS**	17,707
24.3	**POINTS PER GAME**	19.5
49.6%	**SHOOTING ACCURACY**	52.0%
3	**NBA CHAMPIONSHIPS**	5
12 TIMES	**NBA ALL STAR**	12 TIMES
3	**MVP AWARDS**	3

beginning of a decade-long rivalry between Bird and Johnson as the two starters tried to one-up each other.

Bird led the Celtics to the NBA title during the 1980–81 season, beating the Houston Rockets in the Finals after the Rockets upset Johnson and the Lakers in the opening round of the playoffs. Bird sent a message to Houston in Game 1 of the Finals. With the game still in doubt in the fourth quarter, Bird took a jump shot from the right side. He knew it would miss, so he raced in and grabbed the rebound, switched the ball from his right to his left hand, and flipped it into the hoop as he fell out of bounds. Boston held on to win the game and the series. "That is the greatest play I've ever seen," Red Auerbach said. "Larry Bird is a player of destiny."[3]

TUG OF WAR

While Bird and Johnson spent the early 1980s raising the NBA's profile, fans waited for the two stars to face off in the NBA Finals. The Celtics fell short in 1982 and 1983, while Johnson made the Lakers fixtures in the championship round. Los Angeles beat the Philadelphia 76ers again in 1982, with the 76ers getting their revenge the following season. In 1984, Boston and Los Angeles finally met in the Finals. Everybody wanted to watch the two stars with the different personalities but similar styles face off. TV ratings, a measure of the number of people watching games, skyrocketed during this era.

Johnson and Bird went head-to-head in the Finals three times. Bird and the Celtics edged the Lakers in 1984. Johnson and the Lakers evened the score in 1985. The tiebreaker came in 1987. The Lakers led the series two games to one, but Boston were up 106–105 with seven seconds left in Game 4. Los Angeles put the ball in the hands of Johnson, who hit a running hook shot in the lane to give the Lakers the lead. Bird's three-pointer at the buzzer missed, and Los Angeles went on to close out the series in six games.

While Los Angeles celebrated its fourth title of the 1980s, the real winner was the NBA. More than 24 million people had watched the series on TV.[4] In the span of a few years, Johnson and Bird had almost single-handedly lifted the NBA to prominence. Their brilliant play set the stage for the NBA to become a global force. The league just needed one more ingredient: a new star to carry it to the next level. Thankfully, one was on the way.

AIR TIME

Michael Jordan's dominance in the NBA cemented his status as one of the greatest athletes of all time.

ohnson and Bird turned the NBA into must-see TV. Yet for all their flash, they played the game below the rim. They brought fans to their feet in many ways, but flying to the basket for a rim-rattling dunk was not one of them.

The game would change again with the arrival of Michael Jordan. Jordan grew up in North Carolina. Baseball was his first love, but he started to play basketball so he could follow in the footsteps of Larry, his older brother. Jordan tried out for the varsity team at his high school as a sophomore but didn't make the cut. A growth spurt between his sophomore and junior seasons changed everything. Jordan shot up from five feet 11 to six feet three, and he eventually filled out all the way to six feet six.

Suddenly, he was big enough to hold his own against the best players around. And while some athletes grew nervous when the spotlight was on them, Jordan excelled. As a freshman at the University of North Carolina in 1982, he sank the game-winning jump shot in the national championship game to give legendary Tar Heels coach Dean Smith his first national title. He helped Team USA win a gold medal at the 1984 Olympics, and he left North Carolina after his junior season in 1984 to enter the NBA Draft.

The Houston Rockets had the top pick that year, and they used it to draft center Hakeem Olajuwon. The Portland Trail Blazers held the second selection. Portland already had a star guard in Clyde "The Glide" Drexler. The team chose

Jordan signed with the Chicago Bulls in September 1984.

center Sam Bowie out of the University of Kentucky. It's a decision that altered the course of basketball history.

BE LIKE MIKE

The Chicago Bulls picked third, and they practically sprinted to the podium to select Jordan. In his rookie season in

1984–85, racing down the court with his tongue hanging out as he thought up his next move, Jordan took the NBA by storm. He averaged 28.2 points, earned the nickname Air Jordan for his soaring dunks, and was named Rookie of the Year.

A foot injury forced him to miss most of his second season, but he returned in time for the playoffs. The Bulls faced Bird and the Celtics in the opening round. Though Boston swept Chicago in three games, Jordan's spectacular play announced to the world that he was ready to be the face of the league. During a double-overtime loss in Game 2, Jordan poured in 63 points.

During the 1980s, the NBA borrowed the ABA's idea and introduced the Slam Dunk Contest as part of the league's annual All-Star Weekend. Jordan lost the contest to Atlanta Hawks star Dominique Wilkins in 1985, but two

The NBA brought the Slam Dunk Contest to the league's annual All-Star Weekend starting in 1984. Over the years, the Slam Dunk Contest has become one of the NBA's most popular events, with rising stars often participating in the contest to show off their creativity. Slam dunk champions through the years include Kobe Bryant, Vince Carter, and Dwight Howard. The event isn't just for big guys, either. In 1986, 5-foot-7 Atlanta Hawks guard Spud Webb soared to victory by passing the ball off the ground to himself before grabbing the ball in midair and slamming it through the hoop.

years later, he was ready to soar. Wearing a pair of Nike Air Jordan sneakers at the 1987 contest, Jordan beat Portland's Jerome Kersey to win the title. What he really wanted, though, was a rematch against Wilkins. Wilkins was known as the Human Highlight Film for his powerful slams, and he was the one player who could match Jordan dunk for dunk. Competing at Chicago Stadium in 1988, Jordan had the home court advantage.

The crowd rose to its feet in the semifinal, when Jordan took the ball in his hands and ran the length of the floor. When he reached the foul line 15 feet (4.6 m) from the basket, he took off. He extended the ball in front of him with his right hand and pulled his legs back. Air Jordan had taken flight. He slammed the ball into the net as the home crowd roared. The judges gave him a perfect score of 50, and even Wilkins nodded in approval. Jordan went on to edge Wilkins in the final. The legend of Michael Jordan was born.

BECOMING A CHAMPION

By 1990, Jordan was one of the most famous people on the planet. He had made a series of commercials for Nike with filmmaker Spike Lee that made him a household name in the United States and beyond. Fans flocked to buy his latest signature shoe. In every NBA city Jordan and the Bulls visited, people packed the arena to watch Jordan put on a show.

Jordan wanted more. The Bulls were competitive during the late 1980s, but they found their path to a championship blocked by the Detroit Pistons. Detroit embraced their role as the NBA's toughest team. The Pistons were nicknamed the Bad Boys for their rugged, physical play. In 1988, 1989, and 1990, Detroit bullied the Bulls, knocking Jordan out of the playoffs in the process.

By 1991, though, Jordan was ready. So were his teammates. Jordan found himself surrounded by players who could complement his talent. Forward Scottie Pippen was one of the NBA's best defenders and could slash his way to the basket when opponents tried to double-team Jordan. Guards John Paxson and Craig Hodges would spot up from three-point range to give Chicago a deep threat. Forward Horace Grant and center Bill Cartwright provided grit in the paint.

The Bulls and their star stormed through the 1990–91 season, winning 61 games. They were even better once the playoffs began. Chicago swept the New York Knicks in the first round and dropped just one game to Philadelphia in the second. The Pistons, two-time defending champions, were waiting in the Eastern Conference finals. Tired of getting pushed around by Detroit, Jordan and the Bulls pushed back. Chicago turned the tables on the Pistons, using their hard-nosed defense to pull off a four-game sweep.

Jordan and the Bulls had to overcome the more experienced and accomplished Lakers, including superstar Magic Johnson, to win the 1991 championship.

To reach the top and become the team of the 1990s, Jordan and the Bulls had to beat the top team of the 1980s: Magic Johnson's Los Angeles Lakers. The Bulls were nervous. Johnson and the Lakers had a huge advantage when it came to experience. Los Angeles had won five NBA titles in the 1980s. The Bulls, by contrast, had never won a championship.

THE
DREAM TEAM

Starting in 1992, NBA players were allowed to suit up for their respective countries in the Summer Olympics. In the United States, the Dream Team was born. The group selected for the right to represent the United States at the 1992 Olympics in Barcelona, Spain, is considered the greatest team in basketball history. The roster included 11 future Hall of Famers, including Michael Jordan, Larry Bird, Magic Johnson, Charles Barkley, Clyde Drexler, and David Robinson. The Dream Team was mobbed by fans everywhere it went during the Olympics. Though the Dream Team players were all stars of their teams back in the NBA, they shared the basketball, making sure everyone got to join in on the fun. The rest of the world watched in awe as the Americans cruised to the gold medal, winning their games by an average of 44 points.[1] While the United States continues to send NBA players to the Olympics, no group has yet come close to the popularity of the original Dream Team. "I don't think you'll see another team like this," said Chuck Daly, the Detroit Pistons coach who helped guide the Dream Team to gold, after the team's final game.[2]

From left, Scottie Pippen, Jordan, and Clyde Drexler celebrated with their gold medals after defeating Croatia in the finals.

Los Angeles took Game 1, but Chicago coach Phil Jackson made a key adjustment before Game 2. He decided to have Pippen, rather than Jordan, guard Johnson. It made all the difference. Chicago won the next four games, including a Game 5 victory in Los Angeles to put the finishing touches on the Bulls' first championship. The final contest showed just how far Jordan's game had evolved. Rather than try to take over the game late, Jordan recognized that Paxson was having a hot shooting night. Jordan fed Paxson down the stretch, with the guard scoring ten points during the fourth quarter to help Chicago pull away.

"[The championship] means so much," Jordan said in tears after the game. "Not just for me but for this team and this city. It was a seven-year struggle. It's the most proud day I've ever had."[3]

"I'M BACK"

The Bulls won three straight titles from 1991 to 1993. Then Jordan stunned the basketball world by retiring after his father, James, died in July 1993. The grief-stricken Jordan decided to step away from the NBA and start playing baseball, his first love. In 1994, he signed a contract to play in the Chicago White Sox organization. The White Sox were owned by Jerry Reinsdorf, who also owned the Bulls. Jordan ended up spending the 1994 season in the minor leagues, playing the outfield for the Birmingham Barons, a team affiliated with the White Sox. Wearing No. 45, the number he wore while playing baseball in high school, Jordan had a .202 batting average with 51 runs batted in in 1994. He went on to play in the Arizona Fall League, where he became friends with future New York Yankees star Derek Jeter.

Though he enjoyed playing in the minors, Jordan's passion for basketball never disappeared. In the spring of 1995 he returned to the NBA, letting the world know by sending out a note that said simply, "I'm Back."[4] Still, he was rusty.

Though he dropped 55 points on the New York Knicks at Madison Square Garden just ten days into his comeback, the Bulls lost in the playoffs to the Orlando Magic.

It was the last time Jordan would lose a playoff series. Chicago put together a record-setting season in 1995–96, winning 72 games, more than any team in league history up to that point. The Bulls went on to beat the Seattle SuperSonics in the NBA Finals. Game 6 was played on Father's Day. As the clock hit zero, Jordan was overcome by emotion. He grabbed the basketball as the clock ran out, ran off the court, and collapsed in tears with his father's memory on his mind. "This was for dad," Jordan said.[5]

The dynasty kept right on rolling. Like they did in the early 1990s, the Bulls won three straight titles. In 1997 they beat the Utah Jazz and stars Karl Malone and John Stockton in the Finals. Jordan provided the highlight moment, scoring 38 points in a Game 5 victory despite playing with a bad case of the flu. Utah and Chicago met again in the 1998 Finals. Late in Game 6, with the Bulls trailing by one, Jordan stripped the ball from Malone. He then dribbled

At the end of the 1998 Finals, Jordan held up six fingers to symbolize his six championships.

up court. He used a crossover dribble to get open and hit a jump shot to give Chicago the lead for good, securing a sixth championship.

It was Jordan's last shot as a Bull. He retired in 1999. Though he returned to play briefly for the Washington Wizards from 2001 to 2003, his legacy will always be associated with his time in Chicago. When Jordan entered the NBA, the league was riding a new wave of popularity thanks to Johnson and Bird. Jordan, however, took the league to another level. While Jordan is considered the greatest player ever, he understood he was a link in a chain that stretched from the beginning of basketball.

"There is no such thing as a perfect basketball player, and I don't believe there is only one greatest player either," Jordan wrote in his book *For the Love of the Game: My Story*. "Everyone plays in different eras. I built my talents on the shoulders of someone else's talent."[6] Now it was time for the next generation to take over.

Yao Ming is one of many international stars who have made a big impact in the NBA.

In the 1990s and 2000s, the NBA became a truly global league. Homegrown stars became known to basketball fans all around the world, and international players made their mark on the league. Players born outside the United States mainland had played in the NBA throughout the league's history. Hank Beenders of the Netherlands, for example, suited up for the Philadelphia Warriors in 1946. But by the late 1990s and early 2000s, the trickle of players from around the globe had turned into a full-blown flood.

The San Antonio Spurs selected center Tim Duncan from the US Virgin Islands with the first pick in the 1997 draft. The Spurs later added guard Tony Parker of France and forward Manu Ginobili of Argentina to the team's mix. They became a core that helped the Spurs win five NBA

Players like Dirk Nowitzki showed that big men didn't have to just park in the lane and stay close to the basket. Nowitzki was just as comfortable behind the three-point line as he was with his back to it. Nowitzki's versatility made NBA teams think differently about what they wanted their big men to do. He made the All-Star team 14 times, won the league's MVP award in 2007, and opened the door for more international players to take their game to the NBA. When Nowitzki was a rookie in 1998, he was one of 38 international players in the league.[1] By the time he began his final season in 2018, the number of international players had risen to 108 players from 42 countries and territories.[2] All 30 teams had at least one player born outside the United States.

titles between 1999 and 2014. The Dallas Mavericks signed a skinny seven-foot forward from Germany in 1998. Over the next 20 years, Dirk Nowitzki scored more than 31,000 points, helping the Mavericks to a championship in 2011. Yao Ming was already a star back home in China when the Houston Rockets selected the seven-foot-six center with the first pick in the 2002 draft.

KING JAMES AND COMPANY

The next face of the NBA after Jordan's retirement didn't come from Europe or Asia. He came from Akron, Ohio, where a high school kid who wore Jordan's familiar No. 23 was drawing comparisons to everyone from Jordan to Magic Johnson to Oscar Robertson as a teenager. The spotlight found LeBron James while he was still playing for St. Vincent-St. Mary High. *Sports Illustrated* put James on the cover of the magazine in February 2002, when James was still a high school junior. The headline on the cover read, "The Chosen One."[3] It showed James with a ball in his right hand while his left hand pointed straight out as if to say, "Look out world, here I come." Though he came from the United States, James would be the next NBA player to become an internationally famous basketball superstar.

James came along at just the right time for the Cleveland Cavaliers. The Cavaliers won the draft lottery in 2003, and everyone knew they would select the six-foot-eight, 245-pound 18-year-old. James gave the Cavaliers and the NBA a fresh face to build around. While the league was filled with plenty of stars, including center Shaquille O'Neal and guard Kobe Bryant of the Los Angeles Lakers, both had spent part of their careers playing in Jordan's shadow. With Jordan gone, the pathway was clear for James's star to rise.

While the league kept going after Jordan's exit, some fans felt the style of play grew stale. Teams like the San Antonio Spurs and Detroit Pistons won by slowing the game down and playing gritty defense. It might have helped them win games, but it wasn't always fun to watch. San Antonio and Detroit met in the 2005 NBA Finals. The hard-fought seven-game series hardly looked like the free-flowing days of Johnson and Bird. The Spurs averaged 84.9 points per game in the series. The Pistons averaged 86.7.[4] The scores were low compared with the 1987 Finals between the Lakers and Celtics. Los Angeles had averaged 115 points during that series, and the Celtics had averaged 111.[5] Something needed to be done to jolt the NBA back to exciting performances.

"SEVEN SECONDS OR LESS"

The jolt arrived in the mid-2000s thanks to a scrappy point guard from Canada and a head coach who ordered his players to play fast. Steve Nash was born in South Africa and grew up in Canada. Nash played college basketball at Santa Clara University in California, then joined the Phoenix Suns in 1996. He left for the Dallas Mavericks in 1998 but returned to the Suns in 2004. He spent his first eight years in the NBA as a player known for his deft passing. Suns coach Mike D'Antoni wanted Nash to do more than just pass. He wanted Nash to run an offense that would boost the NBA into the twenty-first century.

D'Antoni put together an offensive strategy he called "Seven Seconds or Less."[6] The strategy had only one real rule. Once the Suns got the ball, their goal was to get a shot up in the next seven seconds. Nash was the perfect conductor of D'Antoni's attack. He would probe opposing defenses, looking for cracks to feed the ball to a teammate. While other teams walked the ball up the floor, Phoenix would sprint. Scoring soared. The Suns averaged 110.4 points per game during 2004–05, more than any other

Nash gained fame as a skilled passer, but he developed into a leader of a fast-paced offense.

team.[7] Nash captured the league's MVP award after leading the NBA with 11.5 assists per game. Phoenix won 62 games, the highest win total in the league. Nash was the MVP again in 2006 as the Suns won the Pacific Division with ease. The only thing Phoenix's style couldn't do was reach the NBA Finals. The Suns failed to bring home a championship using their fast-paced strategy, but it provided a blueprint for the way the game was evolving.

"I don't think we thought we were the future," Nash said. "I just think we thought we were playing the way that our roster had the best chance to succeed. With a thin creative point guard and no traditional center, walking the ball up

the court and getting in a wrestling match is not going to
suit us."[8]

SPLASH!

Two of the biggest superstars of the NBA in the 2010s were
from the United States but gained a global following. Steph
Curry and Klay Thompson both grew up around the NBA.
Curry's father, Dell, spent 16 seasons as one of the NBA's
first true three-point specialists. Thompson's father, Mychal,
played center for 13 seasons, at one point winning two NBA
titles with the Los Angeles Lakers as the backup behind

THREE FOR ALL

When the NBA adopted the three-point line in 1979, some teams
considered the shot not worth the risk. Boston Celtics guard Chris Ford
made the first three-pointer in NBA history that year. Teams didn't rush
to take threes. The San Diego Clippers made 177 three-pointers during
that entire first season, as coaches were slow to warm to the new shot.

The "Seven Seconds or Less" Suns showed how much of an
impact the three-pointer could make. The 2004–05 Suns made 796
three-pointers. The shot became one of the most important weapons
in basketball. D'Antoni had moved from Phoenix to Houston by the late
2010s, and he found a willing shooter in guard James Harden. Known
as "The Beard" because of his trademark facial hair that reached well
below his chin, Harden loved to let it fly. During the 2018–19 season,
Harden shot 1,028 three-pointers, the most by any player in a single
season in NBA history.[9] Harden made 378 of his three-point attempts.
That's a lot, but it's not the record thanks to the accuracy of Steph
Curry, who made more three-pointers on fewer attempts.

Curry amazed fans with his accurate three-point shooting.

Kareem Abdul-Jabbar. Both fathers had solid NBA careers. Yet the second generation would eclipse their fathers to become some of the modern NBA's top stars.

The Golden State Warriors saw enough of Curry during his time at Davidson College to make him the seventh overall pick in the 2009 draft. The Warriors selected Thompson out of Washington State two years later. Curry and Thompson built a reputation as two of the best young players in the league. When the Warriors hired Steve Kerr to be the team's head coach in 2014, he put in an offense that focused on constant movement. He wanted to create space to let Curry and Thompson do what they do best: shoot the ball.

With their best players taking and making open shots, the Warriors soared. Golden State went 67–15 in Kerr's first year on the job in 2014–15. Curry and Thompson finished off James and the Cavaliers in six games in the 2015 Finals, completing their rise from being the sons of NBA veterans to becoming NBA stars themselves. The greatness of Curry and Thompson was recognized not just in the United States but around the world. At the peak of their success, both players' jerseys were among the top-selling pieces of merchandise in China.

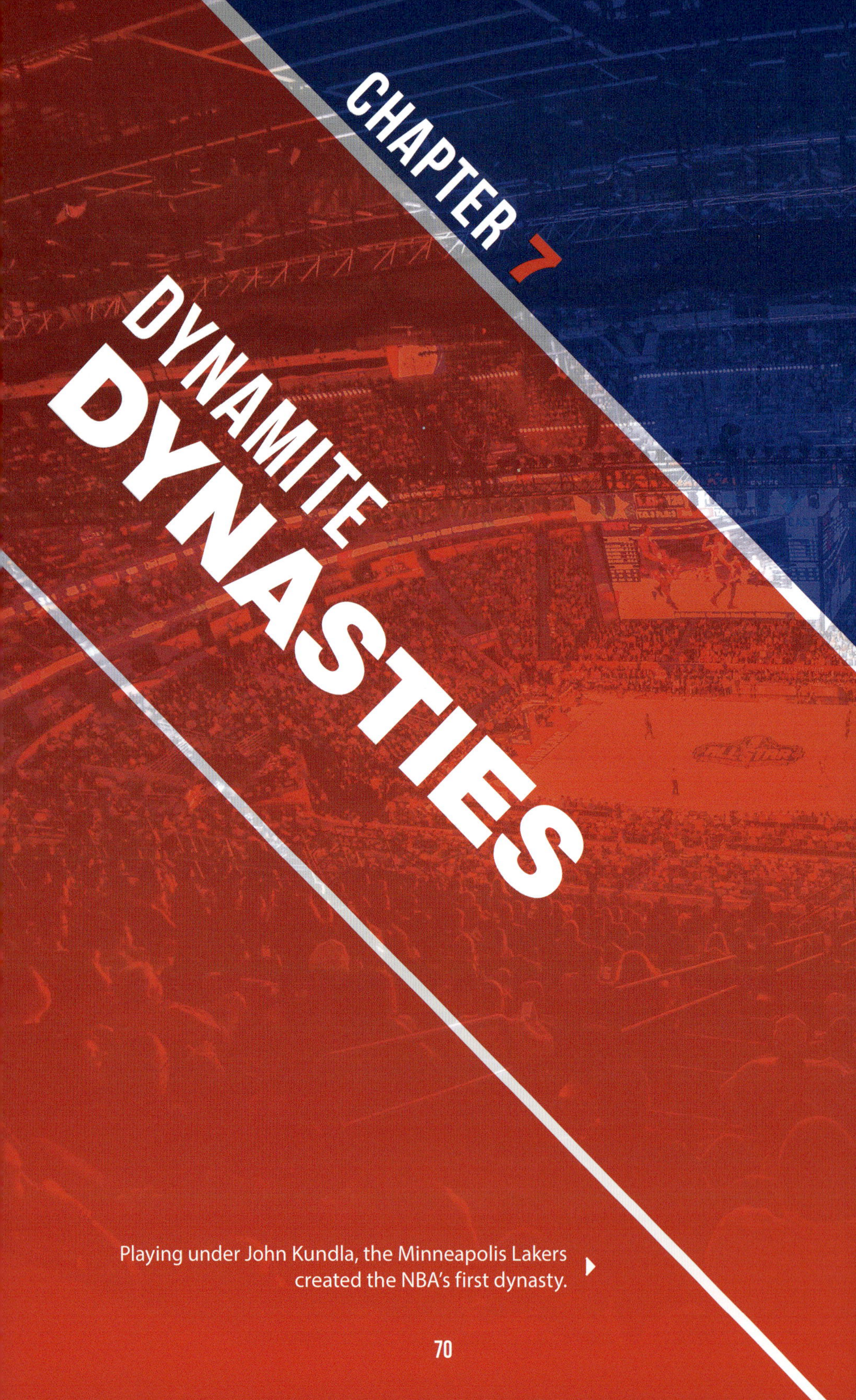

Playing under John Kundla, the Minneapolis Lakers created the NBA's first dynasty.

LAKERS
99

Some teams catch lightning in a bottle and ride the incredible performances by their stars to glory. Bob Pettit of the Saint Louis Hawks poured in 50 points in Game 6 of the 1958 NBA Finals to hand the Boston Celtics a rare Finals defeat during the Red Auerbach era. Golden State forward Rick Barry and his underhanded free throws lit up the Washington Bullets in the 1975 Finals. Dirk Nowitzki's unstoppable stepback jumpers upset Miami's Big Three— LeBron James, Dwyane Wade, and Chris Bosh—in 2011. Each of those champions provided memorable moments, but the success didn't last. By the next season, another team had risen to the top. Some teams, however, found a way to win again and again. Every year during the playoffs, an opponent would rise up and try to take their crown away. And each year the champions would find a way to come out on top again, becoming legends in the process.

THE EARLY GIANTS

George Mikan's hook shots served as the center of the Minneapolis Lakers' offense from 1948 to 1954. The Lakers, though, had far more than just a star center while winning five championships in six seasons. Led by coach John Kundla, the Lakers were the NBA's first super team. Mikan, guard Slater Martin, and forwards Vern Mikkelsen and Jim Pollard all ended up in the Hall of Fame. Martin became an expert at getting the ball to Mikan, Mikkelsen, and Pollard near the basket. Martin was also an excellent defender, bottling up opponents with his speed and intensity.

There was no secret to what the Lakers were going to do. Martin would bring the ball up. Mikan would set up in the post. When Martin dropped the ball inside to his teammate, Mikan would take a hook shot with either hand that opponents couldn't stop. "He was so overpowering, there were no centers around in those days who could cope with him," Celtics guard Bob Cousy remembered.[1] As a result, nobody could cope with the Lakers.

BOSTON IS BEST

Dynasties typically rely on a handful of key players, and when those players retire or move on, the dynasty ends. That didn't happen with the Boston Celtics in the 1950s and 1960s as the team won an astounding 11 titles in 13 seasons. When one of Red Auerbach's stars would get old or step away, Auerbach was ready with a replacement who could keep the machine rolling along.

Take forward John Havlicek. The Celtics were the defending champions and had plenty of stars on their team heading into the 1962 draft, where Boston had the seventh overall pick. The first six teams passed on the six-foot-five guard/forward out of Ohio State. Auerbach pounced at the chance to bring Havlicek in. Havlicek's arrival allowed the Celtics to keep raising banners to the rafters at Boston

Garden even as his older teammates, such as Cousy and forward Tommy Heinsohn, retired. Havlicek ended up joining Cousy and Heinsohn in the Hall of Fame and helped Boston win two more titles in the 1970s before moving on.

SHOWTIME

Magic Johnson put the "show" in the "Showtime" Lakers. Yet Johnson wasn't throwing no-look passes to just anybody during the 1980s as Los Angeles won five championships. There was center Kareem Abdul-Jabbar and his patented "sky hook" in the middle. Forward James Worthy became a Hall of Famer because of his hard work at both ends of the floor. Worthy was a terrific defender who could also slash his way to the basket with ease. Guard Byron Scott was one of the first NBA players to embrace the three-point shot. Michael Cooper provided some toughness on defense. Kurt Rambis didn't look like a typical basketball player with his thick glasses, but his hustle provided a spark for the team.

BOSTON IS BEST 2.0

Larry Bird's creativity found its perfect match in power forward Kevin McHale during Boston's resurgence in the 1980s, when the Celtics raised three more championship banners to the rafters at

The Lakers spent most of the 1960s and early 1970s playing second fiddle to the Celtics and the New York Knicks. In 1971–72, though, Jerry West and Wilt Chamberlain helped the Lakers put together a season unlike any in NBA history. Los Angeles won a then record 69 games that year, a number the team hit thanks to a 33-game winning streak, the NBA's longest ever. The streak began on November 5, 1971, and ran through January 7, 1972. Los Angeles didn't just win the games; they dominated them. Eight times during the streak the Lakers won by at least 20 points, including a 44-point blowout. Only twice during the record run was a game decided by five points or fewer. With 35-year-old Chamberlain in the middle and 33-year-old West and 28-year-old Gail Goodrich knocking down shots from the outside, the Lakers lost just three games during their entire playoff run, beating the Knicks in five games in the Finals.

Boston Garden. While Bird's imaginative passing always kept opponents off balance, McHale kept things basic. He was a true back-to-the-basket player, meaning he was comfortable setting up in the post and going at opponents with a variety of moves in the paint. Boston won the first of their three titles in the 1980s during McHale's rookie season in 1980–81. McHale's star rose as the 1980s wore on. He made the All-Star team seven times on his way to the Hall of Fame. McHale and Bird were joined in the frontcourt by seven-foot center Robert Parish. Parish was known for his quiet nature. The player known as "The Chief" didn't need to speak. He let his actions do the talking for him while serving as Boston's defensive anchor.

THE BULLS DOMINATE THE 1990s

Like the Celtics of the 1950s and 1960s, the Bulls were able to replace players around Jordan and Pippen and keep right on going. During Jordan's brief retirement to play baseball in 1993–94, forward Toni Kukoc arrived from Croatia. When Jordan returned to play, Kukoc had developed into a reliable scorer and a gifted passer. Chicago also brought in spindly forward Dennis Rodman in 1995. Rodman was the best rebounder of his era and was well-known for his colorful personality. He would sometimes dye his hair various colors and liked to wear outrageous outfits. Once he was on the court, though, Rodman was all business. Though he was just six feet seven, Rodman used his long arms and his relentless energy to get the ball. When John Paxson retired in 1994, the Bulls used Steve Kerr as the team's designated spot-up shooter who made opponents pay when they focused on Pippen and Jordan.

SHAQ, KOBE, AND THE LAKE SHOW

When Jordan retired in 1999, it left the door open for a new team to smash through. The Lakers did it behind center Shaquille O'Neal and guard Kobe Bryant. When coach Phil Jackson left the Bulls for Los Angeles, the Lakers took off. Jackson helped his two stars find a way to play together, and the roster was filled with veteran players like sharp-shooting forward Glen Rice and point guards Derek Fisher and Brian Shaw. The Lakers won three straight titles from 2000 to 2002. O'Neal left for Miami in a trade in 2004, but Jackson and Bryant stuck around. The Lakers won two more championships in 2009 and 2010 with a different core around Bryant. Center Pau Gasol from Spain worked in the middle, while versatile forward Lamar Odom, acquired in the trade that sent O'Neal to the Heat, gave Bryant a reliable running mate.

SAN ANTONIO'S SUSTAINED EXCELLENCE

The Spurs during the Tim Duncan era never won back-to-back titles during their run from 1999 to 2014. Instead, San Antonio head coach Gregg Popovich found a way to have his club play with sustained excellence for 15 years. The Spurs already had a star big man in center David Robinson when Duncan arrived in 1997. The two led San Antonio to their first title in 1999. A second title followed in 2003, sending Robinson into retirement a champion. The Spurs retooled and kept right on going. Left-handed shooting guard Manu Ginobili and point guard Tony Parker helped San Antonio reach the top again in 2005 and 2007. The trio waited seven more years before cutting down the nets again. After losing to LeBron James, Dwyane Wade, Chris Bosh, and the Miami Heat in seven games in the 2013

Kobe Bryant (8) and Shaquille O'Neal had a sometimes-contentious relationship, but they enjoyed sustained success in Los Angeles.

Finals, the Spurs got their revenge the next season, crushing Miami in five games in the 2014 Finals behind their aging but still productive stars.

MIAMI AND THE BIG THREE

The decision by James and Bosh to leave Cleveland and Toronto to join forces with Wade in Miami briefly turned the Heat into villains. Some fans and critics rooted against Miami because they felt Bosh and James had betrayed the clubs that drafted them. Their arrival in Miami to create a group known as the Big Three got off to a bumpy start. Miami reached the Finals in 2011 but lost to the Dallas Mavericks in six games. The Heat rebounded quickly. With Wade agreeing to take a backseat as James became the team's focal point, the Heat found their rhythm. Miami cruised to titles in 2012 and 2013. The Heat's run ended with a loss to San Antonio in the 2014 Finals, and James headed back to Cleveland that summer in hopes

of bringing the Cavaliers
a title.

A GOLDEN RUN

Like the Heat of the early
2010s, Kevin Durant's arrival
in Golden State in 2016
created a new Big Three
that made the Warriors
overwhelming favorites to
win a championship. Yet
for all of the points Golden
State put up on a regular
basis, the Warriors were
also a talented defensive
team. Undersized center Draymond Green provided
some toughness in the middle, with guard/forward Andre
Iguodala and guard Shaun Livingston giving a lift off the
bench. Veteran forward David West joined the team in 2016.
West had been a two-time All-Star earlier in his career. He
took on a small but important role in Golden State after the
Warriors parted with center Andrew Bogut before the 2016
season. Like Green, West wasn't particularly big at six feet
nine, but his basketball smarts made him effective on both
ends of the floor. He helped the Warriors win it all in 2017
and 2018 before heading into retirement.

Dynasties are tougher to assemble now than they were in the 1950s and 1960s due to the salary cap. Starting in 1984, teams were given a limit to how much they could spend on salaries every year. That made it difficult for great teams to stay together because the stars command such expensive contracts. The rules have changed slightly over the years. Teams are allowed to go over the salary cap but must pay a penalty known as the luxury tax.

CHAPTER 8

COACHING GREATS

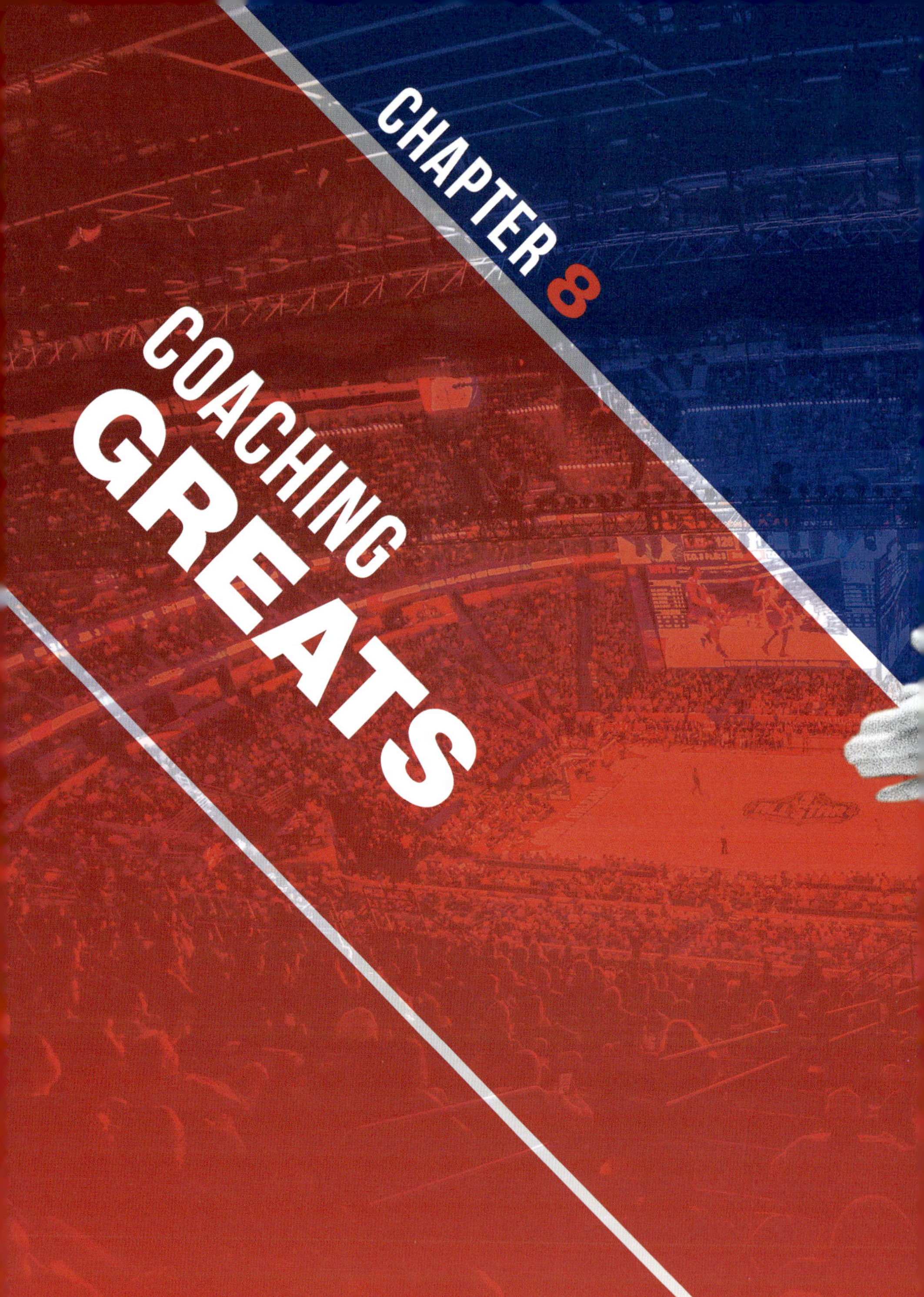

Longtime Knicks coach Red Holzman led his team to two championships in the 1970s.

As great as the players are in the NBA, they still rely on a leader on the sidelines to set the strategy and make big-picture plans for victory. Coaches have been a part of the game since it was invented. Coaches figure out the lineups and try to find a way to keep their teams focused. That's easier said than done during long 82-game seasons and lengthy playoff runs that can stretch on for weeks. The best coaches, like the best teachers, find ways to keep things fresh and help their teams hang in there when the going gets tough.

OLD-SCHOOL MASTERS

John Kundla was just 31 when he was hired to lead the Minneapolis Lakers in 1947, making him barely older than the players he coached. Kundla made sure his players were disciplined and focused on doing the things necessary to win instead of trying to pump up their own statistics. Those rules went for everyone, including Mikan. "John wasn't a screamer and was very mild-mannered, but he'd let loose when we deserved it, and usually I was the first one he bawled out," Mikan said. "The message he sent was that no one on the team was above criticism."[1]

Kundla's influence spread beyond the court. The Lakers did not stay at hotels that did not allow African Americans to stay there, and when he went on to coach at the University of Minnesota, he recruited the first black players to the school. Kundla posted a 423–302 record with the Lakers between 1949 and 1959, capturing five titles in the process.

HOLZMAN'S HEROES

Some coaches drew up complicated schemes to gain an advantage. Not William "Red" Holzman. He simply wanted his players to play defense, move without the ball, and pass it to the open man. His best teams did all three with grace and unselfishness. Holzman coached 18 seasons in the NBA, including 14 with the New York Knicks from 1967 to 1982. The Knicks won championships in 1970 and 1973 with Holzman watching from the bench.

"Red always told us, 'On offense, you guys can do what you want. But on defense, you do what I want,'" said New York Knicks center Willis Reed. "That meant hard work on defense, deny the ball, don't give up the easy shot."[2]

Holzman trusted his players to do their jobs. It led to one of the most famous decisions in NBA history. The Knicks and the Los Angeles Lakers battled to a seventh game during the 1970 NBA Finals. Reed was dealing with a thigh injury. Nobody was sure if he would be able to play. Instead of forcing Reed to play, Holzman left the decision up to his big man. Reed limped onto the court at Madison Square Garden with Holzman at his side as the crowd roared. Reed hit a few shots, but his strong defense also helped keep Chamberlain and the Lakers at bay. His play gave the Knicks an emotional boost that helped them win it all.

ALL RILED UP

With his slicked-back hair and designer suits, Pat Riley made coaching look fashionable during a career that began with the Los Angeles Lakers in 1982 and ran through 2008 with the Miami Heat. Riley won everywhere he went, though his greatest triumph came while helping Johnson run the "Showtime" Lakers during the 1980s.

Underneath his calm demeanor was a fierce competitor. Riley once said, "There's winning and there's misery."[3] Luckily for Riley, he wasn't often miserable. During his 20-plus years on the sideline, Riley-coached teams missed the playoffs

only three times. While Riley coached teams filled with stars, he had a unique ability to get them to work together.

PHIL'S THRILLS

Some coaches hand out game plans to their players. Phil Jackson handed out books, often ones that had nothing to do with basketball. Jackson was just as concerned about how his players approached the game as he was about how they played it. That was just one of the many ways Jackson was different than other coaches of his era. Jackson had grown up in Montana and played basketball at the University of North Dakota before spending time as a player in the NBA in the 1960s and 1970s, mostly for the New York Knicks. He studied Knicks coach Red Holzman closely. Jackson liked the way Holzman kept the game simple for his players.

Phil Jackson oversaw dynasties in both Chicago and Los Angeles.

It's a philosophy Jackson leaned on when he made the transition from player to coach. The Chicago Bulls promoted him to head coach in 1989, asking him to find a way to help Michael Jordan get the Bulls over the hump and win an NBA title. He brought in a style of play known as the triangle offense that forced his players, even Jordan, to share the basketball. It worked wonders, first with the Bulls during the 1990s and then with the Lakers in the 2000s. He broke Auerbach's record for most championships in 2009 when he won his tenth and added one more the following season to bring his total to 11. It was an impressive feat for someone who once said he would never get into coaching.

PROUD "POP"

Gregg Popovich wanted to know what he was getting into. So before the 1997 draft, he flew from San Antonio to Saint Croix in the US Virgin Islands to talk to Tim Duncan, who was the obvious top choice in the draft. Over the course of several days, Popovich and Duncan began a bond that led the Spurs to one of the greatest runs of extended success ever. The trip also showed a side of Popovich that most fans did not get to see. Popovich could be gruff on the sidelines, but he could be tender off the court. His relationship with Duncan was the center the Spurs built around. The relationship served as the cornerstone of an unlikely dynasty. Popovich's secret was that he promised to be honest with his players no matter what, even if that meant the player didn't like him.

"You need to have the same standards for everyone," Popovich said. "You can treat people differently because each one is different, but they all have to march to the same drummer, to the same standards."[4]

KERR'S CLIMB

Steve Kerr played alongside some of the greatest players ever in Michael Jordan and Tim Duncan. It allowed him to watch how coaches like Phil Jackson and Gregg Popovich handled their stars. Kerr brought their wisdom with him when he took over the Golden State Warriors in 2014. The Warriors had been great before Kerr's arrival, but he immediately turned them into champions. He is the only coach in NBA history to reach the NBA Finals in each of his first five seasons on the bench.

CHAPTER 9

RECORD BREAKERS

A famous photo captured Chamberlain in the locker room after his record-smashing 100-point game.

100

Wilt Chamberlain didn't want the ball. His Philadelphia Warriors teammates, however, wouldn't stop passing it to their superstar center. It's hard to blame them. Chamberlain was so hot on March 2, 1962, that the fans in the stands at Hershey Sports Arena in Hershey, Pennsylvania, were chanting "Give it to Wilt! Give it to Wilt!" every time the Warriors came to the floor.[1]

The New York Knicks were playing that night without starting center Phil Jordan, who was sick. That left the task of trying to guard the seven-foot-one Chamberlain to backups Darrall Imhoff and Cleveland Buckner. They didn't have a chance. Chamberlain poured in 23 points in the first quarter. By halftime he was up to 41. He tossed in 28 more in the third quarter to give him 69.

Chamberlain wasn't done yet. His teammates wouldn't let him stop there. As the crowd of 4,124 roared, Chamberlain kept shooting.[2] And the ball kept going in. The Knicks tried double-teaming and triple-teaming Chamberlain and still couldn't stop him. He scored 31 more points in the fourth quarter, including a finger-roll layup in the final minutes that gave him an even 100. The record still stands as the most points by a player in an NBA game. Chamberlain made 36 of 63 field goal attempts and 28 of 32 free throws, an incredible number considering he averaged just over half of his career free-throw attempts. Chamberlain was a little bit embarrassed by his success. "He wanted to come out of the game," Philadelphia teammate Al Attles said. "[Our coach] kept him in the game. Wilt was very careful. He didn't want to rub it in. He was very conscious of that."[3]

HOT STREAKS

Chamberlain might have put together the greatest scoring performance in NBA history, but even he couldn't match what Golden State's Klay Thompson did in the third quarter against the Sacramento Kings in 2015. Over the course of 12 minutes, Thompson scored 37 points, the most ever in a single quarter. Thompson made all 13 of his shots, including

John Long drives the ball on the way to his 41-point total in the record-setting game of December 13, 1983.

all nine three-pointers he attempted. Thompson called his outburst "crazy."[4]

The Denver Nuggets and Detroit Pistons decided not to play much defense on December 13, 1983. The high-flying Nuggets scored 184 points. And somehow they lost by two in triple-overtime as Detroit won 186–184. The 370 combined points marked the most ever by two teams.[5] Four different players scored at least 40 points. Detroit's Isiah Thomas had 47, and teammate John Long notched 41. Kiki Vandeweghe led all scorers with 51 points, while Alex English finished with 47. They didn't reach that total by throwing up three-pointers. The teams took only four threes

ALL-TIME LEADERS

GAMES PLAYED

1. Robert **PARISH**
2. Kareem **ABDUL-JABBAR**
3. Vince **CARTER**
4. Dirk **NOWITZKI**
5. John **STOCKTON**

POINTS

1. Kareem **ABDUL-JABBAR**
2. Karl **MALONE**
3. LeBron **JAMES**
4. Kobe **BRYANT**
5. Michael **JORDAN**

STEALS

1. John **STOCKTON**
2. Jason **KIDD**
3. Michael **JORDAN**
4. Gary **PAYTON**
5. Maurice **CHEEKS**

BLOCKS

1. Hakeem **OLAJUWON**
2. Dikembe **MUTOMBO**
3. Kareem **ABDUL-JABBAR**
4. Mark **EATON**
5. Tim **DUNCAN**

that night, making just two. "I think it's one of those records that will never be broken," Pistons guard Kelly Tripucka said. "I put it up there with Wilt Chamberlain scoring 100 points."[7]

PASSING FANCY

The assist might be the most unselfish act on a basketball court. It means you willingly give up the ball to a teammate, with the teammate turning the pass into a basket. No player in NBA history proved to be as unselfish as John Stockton of the Utah Jazz. Stockton played for the Jazz for nearly 20 years from 1984 to 2003, joining forces with power forward Karl "Mailman" Malone to become one of the most potent one-two combinations ever.

Stockton recorded 15,806 assists over the course of his career, nearly 4,000 more than second-place Jason Kidd, who collected 12,091 from 1994 to 2013. Stockton broke Magic Johnson's record for career assists in 1995 and kept right on going. Not bad for a player who says he didn't think he'd make the NBA after being selected in the 1984 draft. Stockton focused on becoming a good passer while growing up because he figured it would be the easiest way for him to get on the court. Stockton didn't just get on the court; he stayed there. He missed just 22 games during his career. He was talented at more than just offense. He could be a pest on defense, too. Stockton's 3,265 steals are the most ever.

THE DEFENSE NEVER RESTS

You don't have to be tall to be a great rebounder, but it helps. Chamberlain is by far the best rebounder in NBA history. His 23,924 boards are the most ever. Yet not every dominant rebounder relied on size to gobble up missed shots. Philadelphia 76ers forward Charles Barkley was listed at six feet six inches tall but admits he was probably an inch or two shorter. Yet his legs were so strong that the player known as the Round Mound of Rebound would leap over taller opponents to get the ball. Barkley averaged 14.6 rebounds in 1986–87 to lead the NBA and become the shortest player to win a rebounding title.

The blocked shot has been a part of basketball for decades, but it did not become an official statistic until 1973, so fans will never know how many times Chamberlain or Russell sent opposing shots flying into the seats. Center

Hakeem Olajuwon is the greatest shot blocker of the modern era. Olajuwon grew up in Nigeria in Africa playing soccer before coming to the United States as a teenager. The seven-footer quickly developed into one of the best defensive players ever. He swatted 3,830 shots during his career and led the Rockets to NBA titles in 1994 and 1995.

A LONG ROAD, A BRIGHT FUTURE

From peach baskets to power dunks, and from set shots to high-flying swats, basketball has changed dramatically since James Naismith came up with a new game to keep his students from getting bored more than 125 years ago. The game Naismith drew up on the fly is now played all over the world, from Chicago to China, Los Angeles to London, and New York to New Zealand.

More than a century after basketball's invention, and more than seven decades after the NBA's founding, the league continues to thrive.

The heart of the game, however, is in the NBA. What began as a small band of teams in the Northeast and Midwest has spread from coast to coast across North America. The best players from all over the world strive to show their skills under the NBA's bright lights. The league's biggest stars have become household names, from George Mikan in the 1950s to LeBron James, Steph Curry, and Giannis Antetokounmpo today. The NBA remains the world's top showcase for basketball excellence.

Significant Events

- Basketball was invented in the winter of 1891 by Dr. James Naismith, a gym teacher at Springfield College in Springfield, Massachusetts.

- The Basketball Association of America (BAA) merged with the National Basketball League (NBL) and changed its name to the National Basketball Association (NBA) in 1949.

- The Boston Celtics made Chuck Cooper the first black player drafted into the NBA in 1950. Center Bill Russell became the first black head coach in the NBA when he became a player/coach after coach Arnold "Red" Auerbach's retirement.

- The NBA's popularity exploded in the 1980s with the arrival of Larry Bird and Earvin "Magic" Johnson.

- International players joined the NBA in large numbers in the 2000s, with every team having at least one international player on its roster during the 2018–19 season.

Key Players

- Larry Bird played for the Boston Celtics while Magic Johnson suited up for the Los Angeles Lakers. They faced off in the NBA Finals several times in the 1980s, and TV ratings soared. The interest helped grow the league.

- Michael Jordan picked up where Magic and Bird left off. The high-flying star, known as "Air" Jordan for his soaring dunks, is regarded as the best player in NBA history. Jordan won six NBA titles with the Bulls in the 1990s and starred on the "Dream Team" of NBA stars that won the gold medal at the 1992 Summer Olympics.

- LeBron James was a star before he even arrived in the NBA in 2003. The man they called "King" James certainly played like he deserved the crown. James's style was a mixture of Magic's and Jordan's, with a dash of Bird's thrown in. He split his time between Cleveland and Miami early in his career, helping both franchises to NBA championships.

- Steph Curry showed that the NBA wasn't just for big guys. The Golden State Warriors guard is considered the best shooter in basketball history. Teaming up with Klay Thompson, Curry served as the backbone of a Golden State team that dominated the late 2010s.

Key Teams

- The Boston Celtics of the 1950s and 1960s put together the greatest dynasty in NBA history, winning 11 titles between 1957 and 1969. Coach Arnold "Red" Auerbach also helped integrate the NBA.

- The Dream Team that represented the United States at the 1992 Summer Olympics helped spread the NBA's footprint all over the globe.

- The Los Angeles Lakers brought the NBA to the West Coast when the franchise moved from Minneapolis in 1960. The Lakers brought a dash of glamour to the league, from the Jerry West and Wilt Chamberlain team in 1971–72 that won a record 33 straight games to the Magic Johnson/Kareem Abdul-Jabbar–led group that dominated the 1980s.

- Jordan and the Bulls controlled the 1990s. The best of the Jordan-led champions may have been the 1995–96 team, which posted a record of 72–10 and steamrolled opponents on the way to a championship that started a run of three straight titles.

Quote

"There is no such thing as a perfect basketball player, and I don't believe there is only one greatest player either. Everyone plays in different eras. I built my talents on the shoulders of someone else's talent."

—Michael Jordan

GLOSSARY

assist
A pass from one teammate to another that directly leads to a basket.

conference
A group of sports teams, usually from a common region, who play against each other during the regular season.

contract
An agreement between a player and a team that determines how much the player makes and how long he will play for the team.

draft
A process in which sports teams select the top eligible college and international players to join them.

dynasty
An extended period of excellence or success for a team.

expansion
The addition of a new team to a league.

field goal
A two- or three-point basket scored on any shot other than a free throw.

flagrant foul
A foul that is judged as unnecessarily rough.

general manager
For most sports teams, the person responsible for all hiring and firing decisions for players and coaches.

head coach

In the NBA and NFL, the highest-ranking member of the coaching staff, the leader of the team.

lane

Located on each end of a basketball court, the lane is the rectangular area close to the basket. There are rules for how long players can stay in the lane before they have to move. The rule is designed to prevent players from lingering under the basket at all times.

merge

To combine or unite without abrupt change.

rebound

When a missed shot bounces off the rim or backboard and any player can grab it.

salary cap

A set limit on how much money teams can spend on player salaries during a given year.

three-point line

Located on each end of a basketball court, the three-point line is the largest arch. Players can shoot behind this line to earn three points instead of two.

veteran

A player who has played many years in the league.

Selected Bibliography

McMenamin, Dave. "When LeBron Swooped In and Changed the Course of Cavs' History." *ESPN*, 27 June 2016, espn.com. Accessed 19 Aug. 2019.

Sohi, Seerat. "How the NBA Was Saved on the Back of a Napkin." *Sports Illustrated*, 28 Aug. 2017, si.com. Accessed 5 Sept. 2019.

Walker, Rhiannon. "'I'm Back': The Day Michael Jordan Announced His Return to the NBA." *The Undefeated*, 15 Mar. 2017, theundefeated.com. Accessed 19 Sept. 2019.

Whitaker, Lang. "The Dream Team Will Never Die: An Oral History of the Dream Team." *GQ*, 11 June 2012, gq.com. Accessed 11 Sept. 2019.

Further Readings

Big Book of WHO Basketball. Sports Illustrated Kids, 2015.

Bryant, Howard. *Legends: The Best Players, Games, and Teams in Basketball*. Philomel Books, 2017.

Hoehn, Jim. *WNBA*. Abdo, 2021.

Windhorst, Brian. *Return of the King: LeBron James, the Cleveland Cavaliers, and the Greatest Comeback in NBA History*. Grand Central Publishing, 2017.

Online Resources

To learn more about the NBA, please visit **abdobooklinks.com** or scan this QR code. These links are routinely monitored and updated to provide the most current information available.

More Information

For more information on this subject, contact or visit the following organizations:

Naismith Memorial Basketball Hall of Fame
1000 Hall of Fame Ave.
Springfield, MA 01105
877-446-6752
hoophall.com

Fans can take a deep dive into the history of basketball at the Hall of Fame. They can check out plaques honoring all the Hall of Famers or grab a ball and shoot some hoops at the birthplace of the game.

National Basketball Association
645 Fifth Ave.
New York, NY 10022
212-407-8000
nba.com

The NBA is the most popular pro basketball league on the planet. Its website features news and information on teams, players, and more.

SOURCE NOTES

CHAPTER 1. THE BLOCK

1. "Top Moments: Warriors Set Record with 73-Win Season." *NBA*, 2019, nba.com. Accessed 20 Aug. 2019.

2. "Iguodala Relives LeBron's Game 7 Block: JR Smith 'Made the Play.'" *NBC Sports*, 28 Oct. 2016, nbcsports.com. Accessed 15 Aug. 2019.

3. Ben Golliver. "The Ultimate Triumph: Ohio's LeBron James Delivers Cavs' First Title." *Sports Illustrated,* 20 June 2016, si.com. Accessed 15 Aug. 2019.

4. Dominic Patten. "NBA Finals Game 7 Most Game Ever on ABC As Cavs Win First Title." *Deadline*, 20 June 2016, deadline.com. Accessed 16 Dec. 2019.

5. Dave McMenamin. "When LeBron Swooped in and Changed the Course of Cavs' History." *ABC 30*, 27 June 2016, abc30.com. Accessed 19 Aug. 2019.

CHAPTER 2. A MODEST BEGINNING

1. "James Naismith." *Encyclopedia Britannica*, 2 Nov. 2019, britannica.com. Accessed 3 Sept. 2019.

2. "Dr. James Naismith's Original 13 Rules of Basketball." *USA Basketball*, 2019, usab.com. Accessed 3 Sept. 2019.

3. Frank P. Josza Jr. "The National Basketball Association: Business, Organization and Strategy." *World Scientific Publishing Company*, Oct. 2010, worldscientific.com. Accessed 4 Sept. 2019.

4. "Our Story." *The Original Harlem Globetrotters*, n.d., harlemglobetrotters.com. Accessed 26 Sept. 2019.

5. "New York Renaissance." *Basketball Hall of Fame*, n.d., hoophall.com. Accessed 26 Sept. 2019.

6. "New York Renaissance."

7. Charles Paikert. "Pro Basketball Floundered Until It Brought in Feisty Maurice Podoloff." *Vault*, 10 Mar. 1986, si.com. Accessed 4 Sept. 2019.

8. Houston Mitchell. "George Mikan." *Los Angeles Times*, 12 Feb. 2011, latimes.com. Accessed 4 Sept. 2019.

9. Seerat Sohi. "How The NBA Was Saved on The Back of a Napkin." *Sports Illustrated*, 28 Aug. 2017, si.com. Accessed 5 Sept. 2019.

10. "1951 NBA All-Star Recap." *NBA*, 23 Aug. 2017, nba.com. Accessed 27 Sept. 2019.

CHAPTER 3. THE BASKETBALL BOOM

1. Ron Thomas. *They Cleared The Lane: The NBA's Black Pioneers*. University of Nebraska Press, 2002. 212.

2. Alan Paul. "An Interview With Bill Russell." *Slam Magazine*, 17 April 2018, alanpaul.net. Accessed 7 Sept. 2019.

3. Paul, "An Interview With Bill Russell."

CHAPTER 4. BIRD AND MAGIC

1. Rick Warner. "Bird vs. Magic: Their 1979 Matchup Took TV Ratings to Still Unequaled High." *Los Angeles Times*, 2 Apr. 1989, latimes.com. Accessed 10 Sept. 2019.

2. "Earvin 'Magic' Johnson." *Basketball Hall of Fame*, n.d., hoophall.com. Accessed 11 Sept. 2019.

3. "Top Moments: Larry Bird Displays Court Instincts on Grand Stage." *NBA*, 2019, nba.com. Accessed 13 Sept. 2019.

4. "NBA Finals TV Ratings 1974–2008." *TV By The Numbers*, 22 May 2009, tvbythenumbers.zap2it.com. Accessed 13 Sept. 2019.

CHAPTER 5. AIR TIME

1. "Dream Team 25th Anniversary." *USA Basketball*, 26 July 2017, usab.com. Accessed 26 Sept. 2019.

2. Mark Heisler. "They Enjoyed The Inevitable: Basketball: Johnson Advises Keeping the Pros Coming After U.S. Ends Its Gold-Medal Quest With A 117-85 Victory." *Los Angeles Times*, 9 Aug. 1992, latimes.com. Accessed 26 Sept. 2019.

3. Sam Smith. "High Five! Bulls Are Champs!" *Chicago Tribune*, 13 June 1991, chicagotribune.com. Accessed 17 Sept. 2019.

4. Rhiannon Walker. "'I'm Back': The Day Michael Jordan Announced His Return to The NBA." *The Undefeated*, 15 Mar. 2017, theundefeated.com. Accessed 19 Sept. 2019.

5. "Emotional Jordan Celebrates Title Victory on Father's Day Brings Finals MVP to Tears." *The Oklahoman*, 17 June 1996, Oklahoman.com. Accessed 20 Sept. 2019.

6. "Legends Profile: Michael Jordan." *NBA*, 2019, nba.com. Accessed 20 Sept. 2019.

CHAPTER 6. THE GLOBAL GAME

1. Jeff Zillgitt. "Dirk Nowitzki Changed the NBA's Perception of International Talent." *USA Today*, 8 Mar. 2017, usatoday.com. Accessed 21 Sept. 2019.

2. "NBA Rosters Feature 108 International Players from 42 Countries and Territories." *NBA*, 16 Oct. 2018, nba.com. Accessed 21 Sept. 2019.

3. Grant Wahl. "Ahead of His Class." *Sports Illustrated*, 18 Feb. 2002, si.com. Accessed 21 Sept. 2019.

4. "2005 NBA Finals Pistons vs. Spurs." *Basketball Reference*, n.d., basketball-reference.com. Accessed 19 Dec. 2019.

5. "2003 NBA Draft." *Basketball Reference*, n.d., basketball-reference.com. Accessed 19 Dec. 2019.

6. Dana Scott. "Amar'e Stoudemire Made The Suns' 'Seven Seconds or Less' Offense Timeless." *AZ Central*, 14 Oct. 2018, azcentral.com. Accessed 22 Sept. 2019.

7. "2004–05 NBA Season Summary." *Basketball Reference*, n.d., basketball-reference.com. Accessed 19 Dec. 2019.

8. Ananth Pandian. "Steve Nash Comments on Suns' Impact on Rockets-Warriors." *247 Sports*, 10 May 2018, 247sports.com. Accessed 22 Sept. 2019.

9. "NBA Individual Regular Season Records for 3-Point Field Goal Attempts." *Basketball Reference*, n.d., basketball-reference.com. Accessed 19 Dec. 2019.

CHAPTER 7. DYNAMITE DYNASTIES

1. Frederick Waterman. "Red Auerbach's All-Innovator Team: 5 Players Who Changed The Game." *Los Angeles Times*, 19 Apr. 1987, latimes.com. Accessed 11 Sept. 2019.

2. "100 Greatest Moments in Sports History: No. 95, Bird of Prey." *Sports Illustrated*, n.d., si.com. Accessed 26 Sept. 2019.

CHAPTER 8. COACHING GREATS

1. Jon Krawczynski. "John Kundla, Former Minneapolis Lakers Coach and Hall of Famer, Dies at 101." *NBA*, 23 July 2017, nba.com. Accessed 23 Sept. 2019.

2. Dave Anderson. "When Willis Reed's 4 Points Won a Title." *New York Times*, 6 May 1990, nytimes.com. Accessed 23 Sept. 2019.

3. Greg Cote. "Pat Riley Reflects on 50 Years in the NBA, How He's Changed And Why He Loves This Heat Team." *Miami Herald*, 17 Oct. 2017, miamiherald.com. Accessed 23 Sept. 2019.

4. Scott Davis. "Gregg Popovich Has a Brilliant Philosophy on Handling Players, And It Exemplifies The Spurs' Unprecedented Run of Success." *Business Insider*, 18 Mar. 2016, businessinsider.com. Accessed 23 Sept. 2019.

CHAPTER 9. RECORD BREAKERS

1. "Top Moments: Wilt Chamberlain Scores 100 Points in 1962 Game vs. Knicks." *NBA*, 2019, nba.com. Accessed 24 Sept. 2019.

2. Donald Hunt. "Fifty Years Later: Wilt's 100-Point Game." *ESPN*, 2 Mar. 2012, espn.com. Accessed 24 Sept. 2019.

3. Hunt, "Fifty Years Later: Wilt's 100-Point Game."

4. Ben Golliver. "Warriors' Klay Thompson Sets NBA Record with 37 Points in a Quarter." *Sports Illustrated*, 24 Jan. 2015, si.com. Accessed 25 Sept. 2019.

5. Eric Neel. "The Big Score." *ESPN*, n.d., espn.com. Accessed 25 Sept. 2019.

6. "From The Archive: 81 for the Books." *Los Angeles Times*, 23 Jan. 2006, latimes.com. Accessed 24 Sept. 2019.

7. Neel, "The Big Score."

8. Patrick Dorsey. "Yearbook, Nov. 20: AC Green's Record Streak." *ESPN*, 20 Nov. 2012, espn.com. Accessed 26 Sept. 2019.

Will Graves

Will Graves grew up wanting to be just like John Stockton. He ended up writing about the players who make no-look passes instead while covering pro and college sports for the Associated Press. An author of more than two dozen books, Graves lives in Pittsburgh, Pennsylvania, with his wife and two children.